BOOK for BOYS

IAN WHYBROW
ILLUSTRATED BY **TONY ROSS**

Hodder
Children's
Books

a division of Hodder Headline Limited

For Jamie Langdon, who really was
First Aider of the Year 2005. It was his
marvellous rescue story that inspired this one,
and his infectiously lively voice (I heard him
speaking on Radio Four) that I tried to capture
in the voice of my narrator, Alan.
Cheers, Jamie – and thanks!

Text copyright © 2006 Ian Whybrow
Illustrations copyright © 2006 Tony Ross
First published in Great Britain in 2006
by Hodder Children's Books

'Nellie The Elephant' Music by Ralph Butler and Words by Peter Hart.
© Copyright 1956 Dash Music Co. Ltd. All Rights Reserved.
International Copyright Secured. Reprinted by Permission.

The rights of Ian Whybrow and Tony Ross to be identified as the Author and
Illustrator of the Work have been asserted by them in accordance with the
Copyright, Designs and Patents Act 1988.

1

A Catalogue record for this book is available
from the British Library

ISBN-10: 0 340 91114 X
ISBN-13: 9780340911143

Printed and bound in Great Britain by Bookmarque Ltd, Croydon, Surrey

The paper and board used in this paperback by
Hodder Children's Books are natural recyclable products made from
wood grown in sustainable forests. The manufacturing processes conform
to the environmental regulations of the country of origin.

Hodder Children's Books
a division of Hodder Headline Limited
338 Euston Road
London NW1 3BH

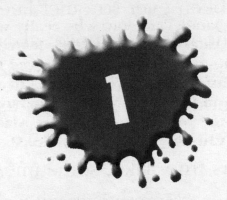

Three Taps

The first time I realized I had super-powers, we were waiting at the traffic lights outside Sainsbury's, me and my step-dad, Raymond. It was a week after he married Mum. They went on holiday. I stayed with my Auntie Rene. Then they came back.

Mum thought going shopping would help me and Raymond get to know each other. I put my ear to their door and I heard her telling him.

"Alan's been ever so quiet lately. I think he might be upset about – you know – us getting married."

Raymond said, "He'll get used to it. You said so yourself."

It was true. Like, sometimes I'd say to her, "Mum, we're all right without you getting married." Then she would say, "Yes, Alan, but I love Raymond and we'll both be better off with a man in our lives. Don't worry. It'll just take a bit of getting used to, that's all."

I put my ear closer to the door. I heard Mum say to Raymond, "Take him to the supermarket, do the shopping."

Raymond said, "I'm no good at shopping."

Mum said, "I'll give you a list. Go on, it'll be nice, just the two of you on your own."

So here we were. The lights were stuck on red. I was thirsty

and Raymond was starting to do that *hrrrm hrrrm* thing he does when he's upset.

I felt my knees under my fingers and I had a thought: "I'm going to tap my knees. I shall start with the left one. Then I shall do the right one. And when I tap the left one again, the light will change."

Then I stopped thinking about it and I did it.

Tap tap tap.

Exactly on tap number three the light changed. Red-and-amber, green.

Da-daaaah!

The Squeezes

At first, I thought maybe that was just luck. So I didn't say anything, I just followed Raymond round the supermarket with the trolley. I was thirsty so I put a can of Dr Pepper in it.

Raymond said, "Better not, Alan, *hrrrm hrrrm*, your mum wouldn't like it." He put the can back on the shelf.

As we continued, I tried sneaking in a Harry Potter cake and a packet of Mars Bars. But both times Raymond said, "*Hrrrm, hrrrm,* this is not on your mum's list, Alan," and he put the stuff back on the shelf.

I didn't say anything but I wasn't happy. So when we got to the checkout, I wouldn't unload anything. I just stood behind the trolley and held on to the bar you steer it with. There was this little baby girl in the seat of the trolley behind. She kept reaching out. She was trying to grab a bag of toffees off the rack next to her. So I thought, "Toffees. Yes. Yes. Yes." And I squeezed the bar of our trolley. Left, right, left.

Exactly on the third squeeze,
exactly, the baby girl got hold of a
packet of toffees.

Her mum said, "Thank you,
Alice. What a good girl. Give it to
the young man."

And she took the packet off
her and put them in my hand.
The baby didn't know what to do,

so she put her thumb in her mouth.
I looked at her mum and I looked
at Raymond. The mum leaned over
towards Raymond and she held
out some money. She whispered,
"Can I get them for your little boy?
Only she won't eat her dinner if I
let her have them."

Raymond went all red.
He said, "No, you're
all right. I'll get them
for Alan." And he did.
And they weren't
even on Mum's list.
Da-daaah!

Nose Bleed

I'm not telling you what team I support. It's not a secret but you probably support Chelsea or something. You'll only say, "Oh, your team's rubbish!" but they're not. Just because you're not in the Premier League doesn't mean you're rubbish. Look what can happen in the FA Cup!

I would have told Raymond, only he never asked me. That's strange, don't you think? If I was somebody's new step-dad, my first question would be, "What team do you support?"

Mum made him come out in the garden with me the day after they came back from holiday. She said, "Go on, you two. Have a kick-about."

Raymond started pulling up weeds and saying things to them in a funny voice, like, "Die, invader!" He likes war games, so maybe that was a war games joke. Anyway, I didn't get it and I just started kicking my football up against the wall.

He said, "Oh, that's good. I'll go in goal, shall I?" He stood between our two apple trees and spread out his arms. I side-footed one to his left. He tried to kick it away but he just scuffed the top of the ball and fell over. "Lucky!" he said, trying to smile and rubbing the mud off his trousers. "Have another shot!"

I dinked one for him to catch. He flapped his hands at it and it smacked him right in the face. His nose started to bleed. "Right, now what do I do?" he said. "Lie down? Stand on my head?"

I hadn't got a clue either, so he went in and Mum sat him down and put a cold wet hanky on his nose.

"You're hopeless, the pair of you," she said. "How come I'm the only one who knows how to stop a nose-bleed?"

Sports Day

Sports Day in our school is rubbish. The day before, Mrs Dreary, our Head, she was up on stage.

She said to us, "Just to remind you, children, there will no cups or medals awarded tomorrow. Everyone is going to take part purely for the fun of taking part. You are *all* winners in my school and that's all that matters to me."

I didn't get it. I like getting a prize if I win something. So I didn't bother to enter for anything, only the long jump. I thought, "I'll use my superpowers and jump *miles*. Mrs Dreary'll go mad! She'll say, "Fantastic, Alan! That must be some sort of record! Why don't you join the Olympic team and do the long jump for England? Then we can tell everybody that you go to my school, St Aphid's!"

And I would look all sad and answer, "Sorry, Mrs Dreary, I can't, because they might give me a medal. And medals are wrong, aren't they?"

I was really looking forward to hearing what she would say about that!

Mum came to the sports field to

cheer me on. She said Raymond wanted to come, too, only they wouldn't give him the day off from work. "Still, he sent you these new trainers and he wishes you luck," she said. I could see from the box that they weren't proper designer trainers. He probably got them off a stall down the market.

I put them on and tried not to look too disappointed because I hate that, when you give somebody something and you know right away they don't want it. "Good fit," I said. I didn't tell her they rubbed at the back.

"What time's your event?" said Mum. She looked at the programme. "Ah. Here we are. *Long jump: starts at 2.35.* That'll give me a chance for a chat with Mrs O'Leary." (Mrs O'Leary is Mrs Dreary's real name, by the way.)

Off she went. I knew she was going to talk about getting married and how worried she was about me going quiet. She was going to ask Mrs Dreary if I was behaving normally in class. Was I getting on with my work? All that stuff.

I danced about a bit to keep warm. Those trainers really rubbed at the back. I watched some of the track races but they weren't up to much. With my powers I could have won them all – but why bother?

The long jump started early for some reason, so there were only two competitors ready, me and this girl with braces on her teeth. There weren't any spectators.

There was Miss Sellers. She was the distance-judge and sand-raker and her friend Miss Riley was supposed to be watching the take-off board. If your toe goes in front of the board, that's it … that's a no jump.

I was wondering who put Betty Lewis's name down for the long jump. I couldn't help thinking that it was Miss Sellers or Miss Riley – maybe both of them. Because the thing about Betty Lewis is, apart from her terrible teeth, she is quite ample. *Ample* is the word we use at St Aphid's for people who take up the whole back seat of a BMW X5.

There was no way Betty Lewis was going to jump over the *board,*

let alone get into the sand. I could
have told anybody that, but I kept
quiet. Anyway, she had a sort of run
at the board. Then she tripped over
it, banged her knee and spat out
her top brace.

So when it came to my jump, Miss Sellers was squatting down drying Betty's eyes, and Miss Riley kept glancing across and sending her messages that she could lip-read, like, "Bad luck, Betty! You *tried*!" They didn't notice me hit the board perfectly and fly about thirty metres. The sandpit was only eight metres long, so I landed in the long grass and weeds by the fence.

I got stung by a stinging nettle, so I had to look for a dock leaf.

"What are you doing over there, dear?" came Mum's voice.

"Aren't you going to come and have a jump, Alan?" said Mrs Dreary, who was with her. "Betty's had a go and done *very* well!"

I walked towards them, twirling a sprig of cow parsley. "I've already jumped," I mumbled.

"Now don't be silly!" smiled Miss Sellers, lifting her rake. "There's not one single footprint in the sand.

Come and have a go, eh?"

They all had such anxious faces!
It got on my nerves looking at
them. And it annoyed me that
Miss Sellers and Miss Riley hadn't
done their jobs properly. So I shook
my head. I'd jumped. They'd all
missed it. That was their bad luck.

Mrs Dreary looked at Mum and
she said something to her. I don't
know if she meant me to hear it,
but I did. She said, "Oh dear. Now I
see what you're worried about!"

Dust Up!

I couldn't see the point of doing first aid lessons after school.

I said to Mum, "There's no point. I've got superpowers anyway." I hadn't meant to tell her the last bit but she forced it out of me, going on and on about me trying for a first aid certificate.

There was a letter from school about it.

"Oh, Alan!" she sighed, and looked at me like I was a sad little baby that had just dropped its ice cream cornet in the sand. "Don't say things like that! It's silly! And besides, you couldn't even stop Raymond's nose bleed."

When Raymond came home, he read the letter and said he wanted to go along as a parent volunteer. "J the J!" he said. Most people would say *just the job*, but not Raymond. "It'll be useful for work, finding out about first aid."

"What, in case you cut yourself on a computer?" I said. As soon as I said it, I got worried in case it had come out too nasty.

"Right!" said Raymond. "You've asked for it!" He crossed his eyes, showed his teeth and shoved me down on to the sofa. Then he started tickling me with one hand while whacking me with a cushion with the other. Every time I tried to get up,

he gave me a right boff and knocked me flat. There was dust flying everywhere. He was laughing his head off and coughing and I started laughing, too. I couldn't help it, it was so funny.

"Raymond!" Mum shouted. "Not too rough!"

As he turned round I gave him a big wallop with one of those sausage things you rest your arm on. Got him! Right round the earhole! "J the J!" I yelled, screaming with laughter at my own joke.

"That's enough now!" warned Mum.

"Only if he gives up!" grinned
Raymond.

"ME give up? What about YOU?"
I jumped to my feet and bounced
the sausage off his head with both
hands. BOFF!

"Alan!" yelled Mum.

Raymond winked at me. "Don't
worry," he said. "She's only a
woman. She doesn't get it!"

BOFF! Mum
donked him
one with the
other sausage.

"Game over!
I surrender!"
laughed
Raymond.

In Off

I was quite pleased to see Raymond next day when he arrived at school. The first aid course didn't start till half past four, so when he came, I was standing on the touchline watching the First Eleven playing Newtown School. Mr Higson was the ref. He coaches the First Eleven.

"Watcher, mate," said Raymond and punched me on the arm. "What's going on here, then?"

I knew he was being nice to me so I gave him a punch back. I felt like sharing something with him. I wasn't sure if I should tell him about my superpowers, in case they went away. Anyway, I said, "See that kid wearing the number 8 shirt, Jason Brick? He's rubbish. He keeps getting offside. He doesn't even know the rules."

"He's like me, then," Raymond said. "It's a mystery to me, football."

"Yeah, well I'm going to make him score," I said. "Watch."

Mr Higson blew the whistle for
a free kick for us, just outside
Newtown's penalty area. They put
all their big lads in a wall in front
of our kicker, Leslie Bass. Jason
Brick was over the far side with
his back to Leslie, yelling something
to the winger. He still had his back
to the ball when Leslie started
his run. I lined up my thoughts
with his paces. Every time his foot

hit the ground I said in my head, "Yes. Yes. Yes. YES!"

Leslie took his eye off the ball, so it spurted sideways off his boot. It hit one of the Newton defenders on the knee and bounced towards Jason Brick. He ducked to get out of the way but it whacked him on the bum. The goalie was diving

the wrong way. How could he
know it was going to thump into
Jason's backside and loop up into
the opposite corner?

GOAL!!

"Told you!" I said to Raymond.
"I made him do that."

He squatted down so his face
was level with mine. He looked
serious and frightened. He said,
"*Hrrrm, hrrrm*, look, Alan. Your
mum and me … you mean ever
such a lot to us. There's no need
to … She told me about the long
jump and everything. I mean, we
want you to just … be yourself.
Be happy. You don't have to … tell
stories."

That was when Mrs Higson,

Head of Year 4, came out. She gave
her husband a wave and said she'd
come to fetch us in for First Aid.
Raymond tried to put his arm on my
shoulder but I wouldn't let him.

The Dummy

I was still in a mood when we got
to the hall. I hated the dinnery smell
in there. I was thinking, "What do I
care about nose bleeds?" when this
lady came in with a suitcase.

She gave us a little talk about
how we could all make a difference
just by finding out a few simple
things. I thought we would start
with pictures of cuts and burns
and broken bones and that, but no,

she said the most important thing in first aid was saving lives.

That was when she opened the suitcase. She took out the top half of a man and laid him on a mat in front of us. Not a real man, but he had hair and eyes and everything. All the kids went, "Errrr!" because his skin wasn't very nice to look at.

The lady said, "This is Jerry. He's unconscious. We're going to resuscitate him."

I thought, "I can't even *say* that, let alone do it! What's she talking about?"

Raymond dug me in the ribs and gave me a look meaning, "I don't fancy that. Do you?"

Bit by bit, she told us. We were going to find out what it felt like to do "the kiss of life". She talked about looking for *signs of life* and airways and circulation and breathing. There was so much to take in! But the lady said there was plenty of time, not to worry, we would get used to it.

I thought, "Oh yeah? I've heard that one before."

The lady said something about DRAB. I know that one now. It means Danger, Response, Airway, Breathing – but then it went straight in one ear and out the other. I was too worried about getting it wrong.

One or two people had a go on the dummy. It wasn't really kissing. You had to put your mouth over his mouth but you had your own little rubber thing that went over the lips,

so no need to worry about other people's spit. Yuck!

All of a sudden, the lady called me and Raymond on to the mat. Raymond lifted his eyebrows meaning, "Who's going first?" I went first. I didn't bother about feeling for the pulse that first time. Just two fingers under the dummy's chin and push his head back till his chin's a bit higher than the point of his nose. Listen for his breathing for ten seconds. Then give him two breaths, not too fast.

"Good. Now the compressions," said the lady.

That meant you had to push down on his chest. And if you sing in your head:

Nellie the **el**ephant **packed** her
trunk and **said** good**bye** to the **circ-us**.

Off she **went** with a **trump**ety
trump. **Trump! Trump! Trump!**
… that makes fifteen "compressions"
and then you give two more breaths.
Only don't do it too fast or you get
dizzy.

Afterwards Mrs Higson came over
and said it was nice of Raymond to

bring me, and well done because he was the only parent to turn up!

Raymond said, "Yeah, well, it was our Alan's idea, really. He gave me a nose bleed the other day and neither of us had a clue how to stop it."

"*Alan?*" said Mrs Higson, looking shocked. "*Alan* gave you a nose bleed?"

"Only kidding," laughed Raymond. "He let fly with a football. I was too slow to get out the way, that's all. He's got a heck of a boot on him!"

"Has he?" came Mr Higson's loud voice. He'd just come into the hall to fetch Mrs Higson home. "Alan, you'd better come and talk to me about a trial for the First Eleven. We're always short of strikers."

"Really?" I said. "OK, then!" I was hoping I didn't look as pleased as I felt.

As I got into the car with Raymond, I suddenly remembered the way he'd said "our Alan", all casual like. And I thought, "I s'pose I am now, in a way."

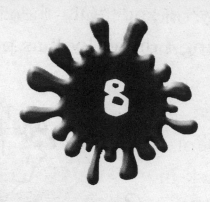

Call an Ambulance!

It was the week my team got into the third round of the FA Cup, against Liverpool. Imagine! *Us* playing at Anfield! Unbelievable!

No point in mentioning it to Raymond, of course. Every Tuesday night, driving home from First Aid, I would try to explain to him about stepovers and offside and that, but it was a waste of time. He did come and watch me playing

for our Seconds, I'll give him that.
And he said he was really proud
of me when I
got picked as a
replacement for
Jason Brick in
the First Eleven
game against
Long Lane. Can
you believe it,
he actually
hugged me!

Things were
going pretty well and I'd more
or less forgotten about my superpowers, really. Anyway, it was a
Saturday morning and I was just
coming out of the newsagent's with
the paper.

I was reading up about my team in the sports section when I saw these three grown-ups standing round an old man who was lying on the pavement. He looked terrible. His face was like cold porridge.

I thought, "One of these people will know what to do," but they all just stood there, looking down.

I said, "Anyone here know first aid?" and I found myself looking round to see if there was any Danger. Was there anything going to make things even worse for the old man or the people near him? No. No traffic? No. Any falling objects? No, all clear.

I didn't even realize then that I was thinking DRAB. Danger is the

first part of DRAB! But I wasn't
thinking that then because it all
happened so fast. I didn't even have
time to think about using my superpowers or anything. I just found
myself saying to the people, "Don't
panic! Because as long as you
panic, you'll attract a crowd and that
won't make it very easy for me."

One of the people said, "Here! Leave off! You can't do any good. You're only a young boy!" I didn't take a bit of notice. I saw this kid I knew on a bike. I said, "Hey! Got a phone on you, mate?" He said yes. I said, "Call 999 for an ambulance!"

I had a good look at the old

man, looking for *signs of life*. Nothing.
So I started talking to him, squeezing
his shoulder but not moving him at
all in case he was injured. I couldn't
find his pulse, his eyelids weren't
moving, nor his Adam's apple,
nothing.

I didn't think about the first aid
lessons. I couldn't. That had all gone
in one ear and out the other – or so
I thought. But suddenly there I was,
lifting up his chin, making sure he
hadn't swallowed his tongue.

Now it's one thing doing the kiss
of life on a dummy, but when
you've got to do it to a real person,
it's not the same. And I didn't have
one of those little rubber things
to put on his lips. But too bad if

he was a bit beery, it didn't put me off. I just pinched his nose, covered his mouth with mine and breathed two steady breaths into him.

His chest came up both times but he didn't carry on breathing on his own. So I felt for his breastbone, put the heel of my hand just a bit higher and locked my two hands together on that spot. That way you

can let the weight of your body press down and you don't have to have big muscles. Off I went singing "Nellie the Elephant" and doing compressions to get his heart and circulation going.

Two breaths, fifteen compressions. It was strange, because I was expecting his chest to make a clicking sound like the dummy's, but it didn't. I was still going at it when the ambulance came.

"Good job, lad!" said the para-medic. "We'll take over now."

There were about twenty people standing around by the time they got the old man in the back of the ambulance. I hadn't noticed. Boy, I was tired!

Surprises

I couldn't believe it when I got
the Young First Aider of the Year
award for my age-group. My
mum had put my name down for
it without me even knowing. I had
to go to London and appear on
"Newsround" on TV and do a radio
interview with a lady from St John
Ambulance and everything. Oh yes,
I was famous for a while. You
probably saw me in the papers.

That was one of the biggest
surprises I've ever had in my life,
but I had another one before that.

It was the Saturday after the old
man collapsed in the street. He was
fine, by the way. He
was diabetic. Mr Curry,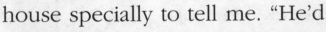
his name was, I found
that out after. He had
what they call a diabetic
coma. The ambulance
crew came round to our
house specially to tell me. "He'd

be dead if it wasn't
for your boy," the
driver said.
Mum started blinking
and her chin went
all wobbly, but it

was *Raymond* who started crying!

Anyway, it was the following Saturday, like I said, and I was having a lie-in.

Raymond put his head round my bedroom door and knocked on the inside of it.

"Knock on the outside, Cheeky!" I growled.

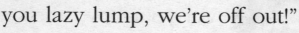

He said, "I'll give you cheeky! Get up and dress yourself, you lazy lump, we're off out!"

I was horrified. I said, "No we're not! We *can't* go out! They're showing the match on Sky this afternoon. My team v Liverpool – not that *you'd* know anything about it!"

He grinned. "Oh, fine," he said. "You stay in and watch it, then. Your mum and I will just have to drive up to Anfield on our own."

"What are you talking about?" I said.

"This is a once in a lifetime thing!" he said. "I thought we'd better go and see what all the fuss is about."

I jumped out of bed. "This isn't funny, Raymond. You're winding me up, I know it! You can't have tickets for the match. They're ..."

"... Gold dust?" grinned Raymond. "You're right there, son." He reached into his back pocket

 and pulled out some coloured strips of paper. He spread them into a fan with his finger and thumb so you could see there were 1-2-3 of them. "Cost me a hundred quid each on eBay!"

Up and Away!

Three hours later we were sitting in a traffic jam on the M6! We heard on the car radio that a petrol tanker had turned over and spilled its load just outside Birmingham. There was a twenty-mile tailback!

Mum turned the engine off. Raymond looked at his watch. He shook his head. "If the kick-off's at three, there's no *way* we're going to make it now, Alan," he sighed.

I was gutted. "C-can't we go another way?" I stuttered.

"What other way?" said Mum. "Look at these cars. We won't even make it to the next turn-off. I'm so sorry, love."

I put my hands on my knees. "Hold tight," I said quietly.

"D'you what, Alan?" said Raymond.

I didn't answer. I just stared ahead and tapped my left knee. Tap. Then the right. Tap. Then the left once more.

Our old Mondeo began to shake like a ride at a fairground. "Hang on to your seats!" I yelled. "We have lift-off!"

Up we went, like a … Well, it was a bit like being in a lift and a bit like

being in a helicopter. Or maybe
more like being in a rocket or a
flying saucer, only there wasn't any
roaring or whooshing. We just went
straight up in the air in complete
silence until the lines of cars looked
like long pencil marks on a big map

with fields all round and cows in them the size of ants.

"Help!" squeaked Mum. "What's happening?"

"Don't panic," I said, as calmly as I could. "Just sit right back in your seats, because we're going forward now, and it'll be fast."

"A-Alan," stammered Raymond. "Don't tell me you've got something to do with this."

"Just look on the map for a place near the stadium where we can land, Raymond," I commanded. "I know you're a bit anxious about me having superpowers. But don't worry. It's like getting married. It'll just take a bit of getting used to, that's all."

Mum and Raymond closed their eyes and held hands. I was so glad they'd found each other. I leaned forward and put my hands on the headrests on the top of their seats.

"I'll do sound effects this time," I called. "Here we go!" I squeezed the headrests. Raymond's. Mum's. Raymond's.

VARRRROOOOM! It was great to hear the roar of a mighty rocket as the car raced forward. What a feeling as we tilted over and raced in a beautiful curve, north west across the wide blue sky!

I had to sing my head off to be heard at all. "Here we go, here we go, here we go!"